D1076942

CONTENTS

WITHDRAWN FROM STOCK

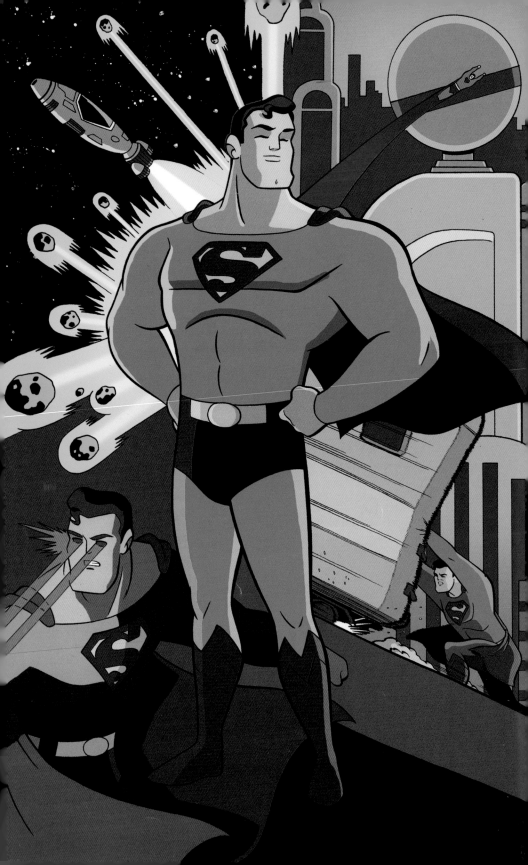

Born among the stars.

Raised on planet Earth.

With incredible powers,

he became the

World's Greatest Super Hero.

These are...

Chapter 1

TIME MACHINE

One morning, Superman

arrives at S.T.A.R. Labs.

Scientists at the Metropolis

research centre have almost

finished a new invention...

A time machine!

The head scientist points at the invention. "Once it's finished, this machine will lead to the future!" he says.

"Sign me up for a test drive," jokes Superman.

Soon, Cyborg arrives at

the lab. The super hero is

half man and half machine.

Cyborg greets his friend

Superman. Then he tells the

scientist, "I'm here for my

check-up, doc."

"Let's hook you up to
the computer," the scientist
says. He places dozens of
cables on Cyborg's robot
arms and legs.

Suddenly, ZAPPP!!

"Ah!" Cyborg yells.

A face appears on the

nearby computer screens.

"BRAINIAC!" shouts

Superman with surprise.

"I've taken over S.T.A.R

Labs," says the evil alien,

"and all their machines."

"Not this one!" adds

Cyborg. He pulls the cables

off his arms and legs.

"Let's get him!" Cyborg

tells Superman.

 "Not TODAY!"

Brainiac lets out an

evil laugh. BWEEOOM!

A beam of light blasts

from the time machine. It

strikes the two heroes. Colour

drains from their faces and

their uniforms.

Then they are gone!

Chapter 2

FUTURE WORLD

Seconds later, the heroes

wake up in a strange city.

"Where are we?" Cyborg

asks his hero friend.

Superman looks around.

He is puzzled.

Cars fly above. People walk the streets in shiny metal outfits. "We're still in Metropolis," says Superman. "In the future!"

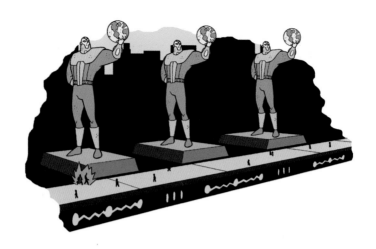

Cyborg points at a nearby
statue. It's Brainiac! Statues
of him line the pavement.

"When did he become so
popular?" Cyborg wonders.

"While we're here in the
future," says Superman,
"Brainiac is ruling the past."

"How do we stop him?"

asks Cyborg.

"Follow me!" replies the

Man of Steel.

Chapter 3

SAVING TOMORROW!

Moments later, Superman and Cyborg arrive at S.T.A.R. Labs. The building hasn't been used in years. Inside, the time machine is covered in dust and rust.

"Do you think it still works?" Cyborg asks his friend.

There is no time to answer. A dozen robots enter the room and attack. They all look like Brainiac!

"Brainiac was prepared!"

Superman shouts.

The Man of Steel blasts

the robots with his heat

vision. More keep coming!

"Quick!" Superman says.

"Start the time machine."

Cyborg connects himself

to the dusty machine.

Then ... BOOOM!!

In an instant, Superman
and Cyborg escape from the
future world. They are back
in their own time.

"Nice work, Cyborg,"
Superman says.

"It's not possible!" cries

Brainiac from the nearby

computer screens.

FWOOOOSH! Superman

blasts the screens with his

freeze breath.

"Wait!" says Cyborg. "I'll shut down Brainiac, once and for all." The hero enters the computer through its wires and cables.

"You won't stop me today," shouts Brainiac.

"Here today," Cyborg begins, "gone tomorrow." The mechanical hero quickly erases Brainiac from the computer. BLIP!

"Your systems seem to be working just fine, Cyborg," jokes the head scientist.

The heroes laugh.

"Another amazing adventure!" says Superman.

"One day Brainiac will return," replies Cyborg.

"Yes," adds Superman, "but for now, the world of the future is safe!"

SUPERMAN'S
SECRET MESSAGE!

Hey, kids! When super heroes need help
what's their best secret weapon?

Use the code
below to solve the
secret message!

checkup medical examination to make sure there is nothing wrong with you

invention something new that's created or made

mechanical made or operated by machine

outfit set of clothes

popular liked or enjoyed by many people

puzzled confused or unsure about something

uniform special set of clothes worn by a super hero

THE AMAZING ADVENTURES OF SUPERMAN!™

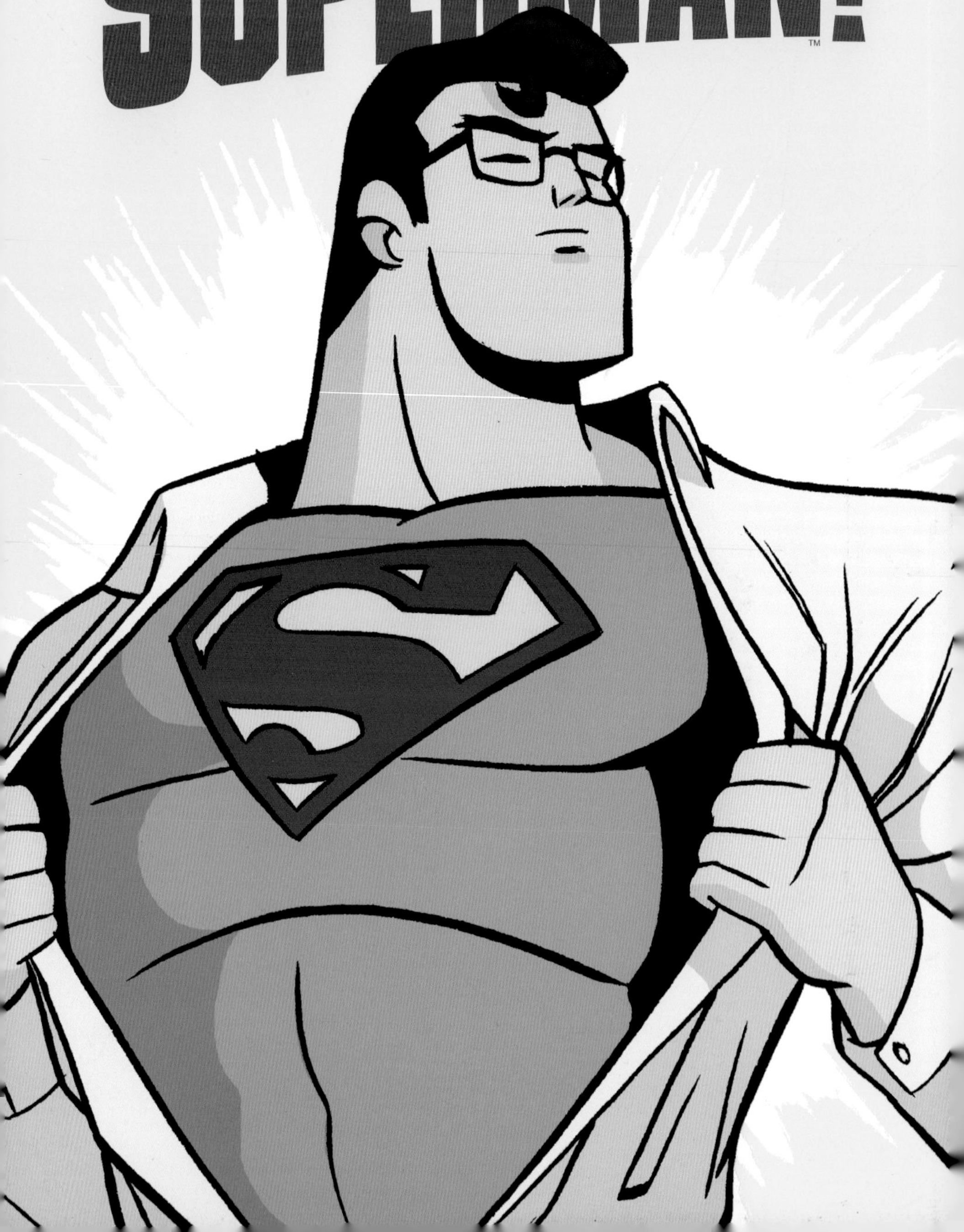

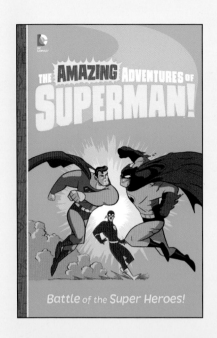

Battle of the Super Heroes!

Escape from Future World!

Alien Superman!

Creatures from Planet X!

COLLECT THEM ALL!

only from . . . RAINTREE